The big-toddlers

My chubby cuddly hungry baby

TEXT Madeleine Allard

ILLUSTRATIONS Hélène Desputeaux

ADAPTED BY Marianne Champagne

ISBN 978-2-923506-36-4

GRAPHIC DESIGN | ARTO design

d e s p u t e a u x + a u b i n

Case postale 235, succursale Beloeil
Beloeil (Québec) Canada J3G 4T1
desto.aubin@desputeauxaubin.com
www.desputeauxaubin.com

WE ARE PROUD TO CREATE, PRODUCE AND DISTRIBUTE WITHOUT SUBSIDIES.

DISTRIBUTORS

Trade Sales: Kate Walker & Company Ltd.
www.katewalker.com

Ordering Information
University of Toronto Press
5201 Dufferin Street
Downsview, ON Canada M3H 5T8
Toll free: (800) 565-9523

General Enquiries & Individual Orders
Second Story Press
20 Maud Street, Suite 401
Toronto, ON Canada M5V 2M5
info@secondstorypress.ca

Legal deposit 2012
Printed in China

My chubby cuddly hungry baby

TEXT: Madeleine Allard
ILLUSTRATIONS: Hélène Desputeaux

desputeaux + aubin

My baby's an explorer.

My baby opens and empties drawers.
My baby plays drums with spatulas,
whisks and wooden spoons.

My baby enjoys dipping bits of paper in the toilet bowl
and lets them dry on the floor.

My baby turns the television on and off during viewing hours.
My baby crawls up on the kitchen table, on the living room
table, on the arms of the settee and on the TV stand.

My baby throws his food around. My baby tips his beaker. My baby explores the cupboard of pots and pans. My baby visits the pantry.

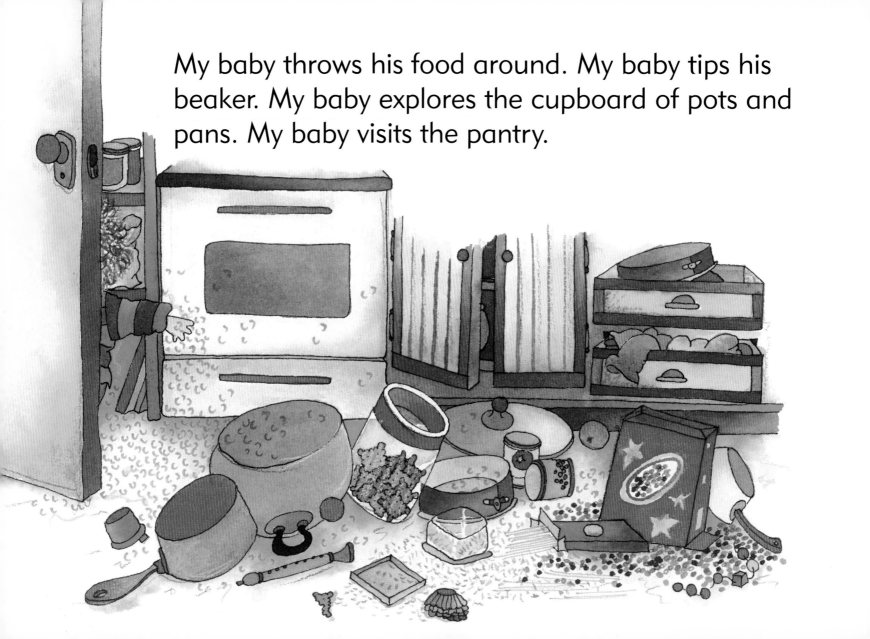

My baby scribbles on the walls,
on the floors, on the furniture, on the bedcovers,
on his arms, on his legs and all over mine as well.

My baby opens, my baby closes, my baby slams the doors.
My baby steals telephones and remotes. My baby slips
his feet in any shoe he finds and leaves it wherever.

My baby drives me crazy.

Luckily, sometimes, my baby takes a break.

My baby's a little glutton.
"Why do you eat all the time?", I ask him.
"Because it's yummy!", he answers.

My baby is such a big eater, with such a big appetite.
"Oh! He does eat heartily, doesn't he?" Granny repeats
constantly.

My baby has a big belly too.
My baby's a big baby.

Before, we used to say:
"He's quite chubby!"
"He's quite pudgy!"
"He's quite tubby!"
Now, we just say:
"He's quite big!"

My baby's still a wee baby and yet he weighs thirteen kilos already. Thirteen kilos of delicious baby flesh.

If I were a cannibal, I'd eat him for dinner. And that would solve my problem of having a baby who drives me crazy.

But luckily for him,
my baby's also very cuddly.

Hugs and tender kisses, my baby gives them happily.
Soft and pudgy in the middle, my baby's quite nice to cuddle.

When he passes right by me, adorable and delicious, I always say: "Come, my baby! Come give a hug! Come give a peck!"

He might resist for a second or two, but always, he dashes and curls up to me.

And then, we're happy,
my baby and me.

We could stay like this
until the end of time.
Because it's yummy.